LAURENCE ANHOLT was born in London and brought up
mainly in Holland. His books have won numerous awards including
the Nestlé Smarties Gold Award for *Chimp and Zee*, the first story about
two lovable twin monkeys which he created in collaboration with his wife,
Catherine Anholt. Among his previous books for Frances Lincoln are
Can You Guess?, *Chimp and Zee*, *Chimp and Zee and the Big Storm*,
Monkey About with Chimp and Zee, *Chimp and Zee's Noisy Book*
(all illustrated by Catherine Anholt) and his Anholt's Artists series:
Camille and the Sunflowers, *Degas and the Little Dancer*,
Picasso and the Girl with a Ponytail, *Leonardo and the Flying Boy*
and *The Magical Garden of Claude Monet*.
Laurence lives with his family in a rambling farmhouse
near Lyme Regis in Dorset.

**For my father, Gerry Anholt,
with love.**

First published in Great Britain in 1996 by
Frances Lincoln Limited, 4 Torriano Mews,
Torriano Avenue, London NW5 2RZ
www.franceslincoln.com

This edition first published in 2003

British Library Cataloguing in
Publication Data available on request

ISBN 0-7112-2157-X

Printed in China

9 8 7 6 5 4 3 2

Visit the Anholt website at www.anholt.co.uk

PHOTOGRAPHIC ACKNOWLEDGMENTS

Please note: the pages in this book are not numbered.
The story begins on page 4.
Paintings and Sculpture by Edgar Degas (1834–1917)
Front cover: *The Dancing Class* (1873–76), Musée d'Orsay, Paris.
Photograph Bridgeman Art Library
Page 5, 13, 26 & 29: *Little Dancer of Fourteen Years* (1880–81),
Sculpture (Bronze and Muslin), Musée d'Orsay, Paris
© Photographs RMN
Page 16 (above): *Group of Dancers* (1890s), National Gallery
of Scotland, Edinburgh. Photograph Bridgeman Art Library
Page 16 (below): *Dancers*, Heydt Museum, Wuppertal.
Photograph Bridgeman Art Library
Page 17 (above): *Dancer Fastening Her Pump* (c.1880–85),
Private Collection. Photograph Bridgeman Art Library
Page 17 (below left): *Dancer at Rest* (c.1880), Private Collection.
Photograph Bridgeman Art Library
Page 17 (below right): *Blue Dancers* (c.1897), Pushkin Museum,
Moscow. Photograph Bridgeman Art Library
Page 31: Portrait of Degas, (c.1890), Photograph Bibliothèque
Nationale, Paris

Degas
and the Little Dancer

A story
about *Edgar
Degas*

by LAURENCE
ANHOLT

FRANCES LINCOLN

*I*n the middle of a big room, in a famous art museum, is a beautiful sculpture of a little dancer. She stands with one foot forward, her hands clasped behind her back. She looks tired and a bit sad.

The sculpture was made more than a hundred years ago by an artist called Edgar Degas.

The guard who looks after the room in the museum has a story to tell about the little ballerina. When it is raining outside and people have nowhere else to go, someone is sure to ask who she was.

"Her name is Marie," says the guard. "I look at her standing there every day, and I think I know her pretty well..."

...Marie and her parents were very poor, but Marie dreamed of only one thing — she wanted to be a dancer. Not just any dancer: she wanted to dance at the Paris Opera House. She wanted to be the most famous ballerina in the world.

Marie's father was a tailor and her mother took in laundry. They worked hard and saved their money, until the day Marie was ready to take the entrance exam for the big ballet school.

Her father made her a special tutu, and her mother wished her luck, and tied a long peach-coloured ribbon in her hair.

At the exam, Marie danced as she had never danced before, and the old ballet teacher seemed to like her.

"If we give you a place," he said, "you will have to practise very hard."

"I know," said Marie, "I want to be the most famous dancer in the world."

Everyone laughed. "We'll see about that!" said the old teacher.

It was the most exciting day of Marie's life. She couldn't wait to tell her family all about it; but just as she was about to rush home, something happened that almost spoiled her happiness.

At the back of the big room, someone started shouting. A girl ran past Marie in tears. She was followed by a fierce, grey-bearded man, dressed in expensive clothes.

"Why can't you keep still?" he shouted. "How can I draw you when you keep moving?"

Marie was frightened. "Who is that bad-tempered man?" she whispered to the girl beside her.

"You will soon find out if you are a pupil here. That is Degas, painter of horses and dancers, and he treats them all the same."

*A*t the museum, a large crowd has gathered around
the statue of the little ballerina.

"Look at her," says the guard. "Look at little Marie.
I'll tell you something – if you stare at her long enough
she almost seems to move!"

"So, did she get her place at the ballet school?"
someone asks.

"Oh yes," says the guard, "she got her place all right.
She worked hard, practising her pirouettes and what-not.
In fact, she became so good that the old teacher began
to talk about giving her the star part in the Christmas Ballet
at the Opera House..."

...Marie's dream was coming true.

And even old Degas didn't seem quite so frightening.
Every day he turned up with his top hat and his sketch books,
muttering and cursing everyone. He worked furiously with
coloured chalks, sketching the girls, the teachers and
the musicians.

"Keep still!" he would shout. "Not like that. Like this...!"

Then he would show some poor dancer how to hold a pose
or to skip properly.

Marie had to try hard not to laugh at the sight of the
smartly dressed painter balancing on one leg.

Sometimes, Marie caught a glimpse of his sketches, and what she saw made her gasp – the drawings almost glowed with colour. There were studies of all the girls, but they didn't look like ballet stars.

Degas had drawn them...

chattering,

stretching,

tying their laces,

adjusting their straps –

even reading
a newspaper.

Marie loved her dancing. She was the first to arrive
in the morning and the last to go home at night.

Then, one day, everything started to go wrong.

Marie's father became ill, and soon he couldn't work
any more. Her mother took in extra washing, but there
simply wasn't enough money to pay for all Marie's classes.

Her dream of becoming a famous dancer began to fade.

"I would love to help you, Marie," said the kind
old teacher, "but unless you have lessons every day
I will have to give the main part to someone else.
Perhaps we could find a little work for you, sweeping
the floor in the theatre or..."

A gruff voice interrupted them. "I will give you
a few francs if you pose for me, but you will have to work
very hard and not chatter. Do you understand?"

So Degas began to draw Marie every afternoon. He made her stand absolutely still for such a long time that Marie almost cried, but she didn't dare to complain.

The money was not enough. It paid for a doctor for her father, but not for the classes Marie needed. As the Christmas Ballet drew near, she knew she would never have the chance to become famous.

When the big night came, poor Marie was not even allowed to watch, because Degas wanted to work late.

While the other girls laughed and chattered and made themselves ready, Marie was left alone with the artist. More irritable than ever, he made her stand, looking up at the ceiling, with her hands behind her back. All the dancers were used to this pose, but as Degas worked on and on, Marie's neck began to ache.

It was getting late.

"Excuse me, Monsieur Degas," Marie whispered.
"I will have to go home soon. My father is ill and my
family will be worried."

"Family!" shouted Degas. "Your family will be worried?
Do you know who will worry about me? No one, that's who.
I have only my work for company and now even my eyesight
is leaving me."

"I'm sorry, Monsieur, I don't understand."

Degas worked in silence for a while. He pulled out
some clay and began to work furiously with his long
fingers. Then Marie saw a tear in the artist's eye.

"No," he said more gently, "how could you understand?
Tell me, Marie, what is the most precious thing to a painter?"

"Your eyes, Monsieur?"

"Exactly. My eyes! Just like a dancer's legs, you understand? And my poor eyes are sick, Marie. That is why I am working with clay, because I can hardly see what I'm doing anymore."

Suddenly Marie felt very sad for the bad-tempered artist. Could this be why he was always angry?

"I am very sorry," she said.

Then Degas did something Marie had never seen him do before. He looked up at her and smiled.

"I am sorry too, Marie," he said. "But look at the sculpture. This will be the best thing I've ever done. Thank you, my little dancer. Now you must go home."

Marie stepped down. Her legs were weak. She untied the peach-coloured ribbon from her hair and gave it to the old artist. Then she put away her dancing clothes and ran home to her family.

In the theatre, the crowds clapped and cheered
as the curtain came down on the Christmas Ballet.
Outside, under a pale streetlight, an old, nearly blind
artist struggled home alone.

In his hand he clutched a peach-coloured ribbon.

"*And so she never did find her dream?*" *someone asks.*
"*Wait,*" *says the guard.* "*The story isn't quite finished…*"

Two years later Marie was helping her mother with the laundry when a letter arrived at 36, rue de Douai.

"It's for you, Marie," said her mother.

Marie tore open the envelope. Inside was a ticket and an invitation to a big art exhibition. On the invitation someone had scribbled 'For Marie, the little dancer'.

Marie and her mother went to the show. The building was very crowded. The walls were hung with brilliantly coloured paintings, but the biggest crowd was gathered around a large glass box.

Marie pushed through the crowd. "Look!" she gasped. "It's me!"

Degas had dressed the sculpture in real clothes. No one had seen anything like it before. In her hair was the peach-coloured ribbon.

*A*t the museum the last person has gone home and
the guard wipes a little dust from the dancer's shoe.
"Good night, Marie," he says, and he walks away,
whistling to himself.
As the keys turn in the lock, the little dancer
almost seems to smile. The rain on the museum
roof sounds like a thousand hands clapping –
clapping for Marie, the most famous
dancer in the world.

EDGAR DEGAS (1834–1917) was born in Paris, the eldest son of a wealthy banker.
As a young man, he studied drawing in Paris and Italy, and soon became well-known
for his pictures of racehorses, his nudes, and of course, his ballet dancers, which made up
half his work. He was also very keen on printmaking and photography.

He sold many pictures, and was a great collector of other artists' work, owning such famous
paintings as Van Gogh's *Sunflowers*. Although he never married, he thought of the paintings
in his collection as his "children".

Degas was a bad-tempered man who upset many people, although he would often apologise
afterwards. He spent hours observing and sketching, totally absorbed in his work.

As his eyesight worsened, he turned from oil painting to large pastel drawings, and began
modelling with wax and clay. In 1880 he asked Marie van Goethen, a young pupil at the
Opera Ballet School in Paris, to pose for him. The finished wax model of *The Little Dancer*,
fully clothed and wearing a real wig, was the only Degas sculpture to be exhibited during
his lifetime. It was displayed in a glass case at the Impressionist Exhibition of 1881, where
its extraordinary realism created a sensation.

The original sculpture of *The Little Dancer* is now in the Louvre, Paris. After Degas' death,
the model was cast in bronze, and more than 20 copies were made. Some of these bronzes
can be seen today in the collections of major museums and galleries around the world.

MORE TITLES IN THE ANHOLT'S ARTISTS SERIES

CAMILLE AND THE SUNFLOWERS

"One day a strange man arrived in Camille's town. He had
a straw hat and a yellow beard…" The strange man is the artist Vincent van Gogh,
seen through the eyes of a young boy entranced by Vincent's painting.

ISBN 0-7112-2156-1

LEONARDO AND THE FLYING BOY

Every day, Zoro the young apprentice, works hard in Leonardo da Vinci's workshop.
But there is one place he is not allowed to go… a mysterious workshop
where Leonardo spends hours working away at a secret invention.
When Zoro manages to sneak inside, he is sent soaring into an extraordinary adventure.

ISBN 0-7112-2132-4

THE MAGICAL GARDEN OF CLAUDE MONET

When Julie crawls into a mysterious garden, she meets an old man tending the flowers.
The gentle gardener turns out to be the great artist, Claude Monet and together
they explore his magical world. Monet and Julie wander across the Japanese bridge,
around the house and studios and they float through water gardens
where lilies sparkle as bright as stars.

ISBN 0-7112-2104-9

PICASSO AND THE GIRL WITH A PONYTAIL

Shy Sylvette is astonished when Pablo Picasso, the famous artist,
chooses her to be his model. As the pictures become larger and more extraordinary,
Picasso helps Sylvette to be brave and realise her dreams.

ISBN 0-7112-1177-9

**Frances Lincoln titles are available from all good bookshops.
You can also buy books and find out more about your favourite titles,
authors and illustrators on our website: www.franceslincoln.com**